The Giant's Causeway

Julie Ellis
Adam Nickel

Nelson Thornes

First published in 2007 by Cengage Learning Australia
www.cengage.com.au

This edition published under the imprint of Nelson Thornes Ltd,
Delta Place, 27 Bath Road, Cheltenham, United Kingdom, GL53 7TH

10 9 8 7 6 5 4 3 2
11 10 09 08

Text © 2007 Cengage Learning Australia Pty Ltd ABN 14058280149
(incorporated in Victoria)
Illustrations © 2007 Cengage Learning Australia Pty Ltd ABN 14058280149
(incorporated in Victoria)

The right of Julie Ellis to be identified as author of this work has been asserted by him/her in accordance with the Copyright, Designs and Patents Act 1988

All rights reserved. No part of this publication may be reproduced or transmitted in any form or by any means, electronic or mechanical, including photocopy, recording or any information storage and retrieval system, without permission in writing from the publisher or under licence from the Copyright Licensing Agency Limited, of 90 Tottenham Court Road, London W1T 4LP.

Any person who commits any unauthorised act in relation to this publication may be liable to criminal prosecution and civil claims for damages.

The Giant's Causeway
ISBN 978-1-4085-0141-2

Story by Julie Ellis
Illustrations by Adam Nickel
Edited by Johanna Rohan
Designed by Mandi Cole
Series Design by James Lowe
Production Controller Seona Galbally
Audio recordings by Juliet Hill, Picture Start
Spoken by Matthew King and Abbe Holmes
Printed in China by 1010 Printing International Ltd

Website www.nelsonthornes.com

The Giant's Causeway

Julie Ellis
Adam Nickel

Contents

Chapter 1	**Smack!**	4
Chapter 2	**Building the Giant's Causeway**	10
Chapter 3	**Oonagh's Plan**	14
Chapter 4	**The Isle of Man**	22

Chapter 1

Smack!

Finn McCool was an Irish giant.
He was big and strong,
and he had won many battles.
But, Finn was tired of fighting.

Smack!

One day, Finn met Oonagh,
a clever giantess.
Finn and Oonagh liked each other,
so they decided to live together
in a quiet cave by the sea.
Finn liked to sit and look out
over the water.
He could just make out Scotland,
far away in the distance.
"There's no place like home,"
said Finn, contentedly.

Smack!
A heavy rock landed near Finn.

"Who threw that?"
roared Finn, jumping up.

"I did!" came a loud voice.
"The mighty Benandonner
of Scotland."

Smack!

"I've heard that the Irish giant Finn McCool is now old and feeble. You call yourself a fighter? I could whip you with one hand behind my back!" yelled Benandonner.

"Come over here and say that!" yelled Finn, angrily. "I'm the strongest giant in this land."

The Giant's Causeway

"It's only the water that's stopping me from coming to fight you,
Finn McCool!"
Benandonner shouted back.

"Afraid of water, are you?"
yelled Finn.

"Afraid? No!" shouted Benandonner.
"I just don't know how to swim."

Smack!

"I'll make a causeway," yelled Finn. "Then you'll have to come over and fight, giant to giant."

Chapter 2

Building the Giant's Causeway

Finn began to pull great slabs of rock off the cliff.
He threw them into the water to make a path.
The slabs were heavy,
and it was a long way from Ireland to Scotland.

Building the Giant's Causeway

It took Finn a week to finish
the causeway.
He threw down the last slabs
late one night, and then
walked back over the causeway
to his cave.

"I'm tired.
I'm going to bed now.
I need to get some strength
before I face Benandonner,"
Finn told Oonagh.

The Giant's Causeway

In the morning, Oonagh woke early. She went outside because someone was making a lot of noise.

Benandonner was walking over the causeway, shouting, "I'm coming to get you, Finn."

Oonagh could see that Benandonner
was much bigger than Finn.
She rushed in to warn Finn,
but he was still asleep.
Oonagh knew that Finn was so tired
he might lose the fight.

Chapter 3

Oonagh's Plan

Suddenly, Oonagh had a plan.
She woke Finn and made him put on
her biggest dress.
Ripping open a pillowcase,
she tied it around Finn's head.
She made Finn lie down
and pretend he was asleep,
and then she put their biggest
blanket over him.

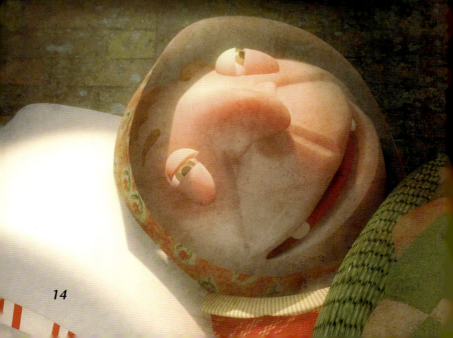

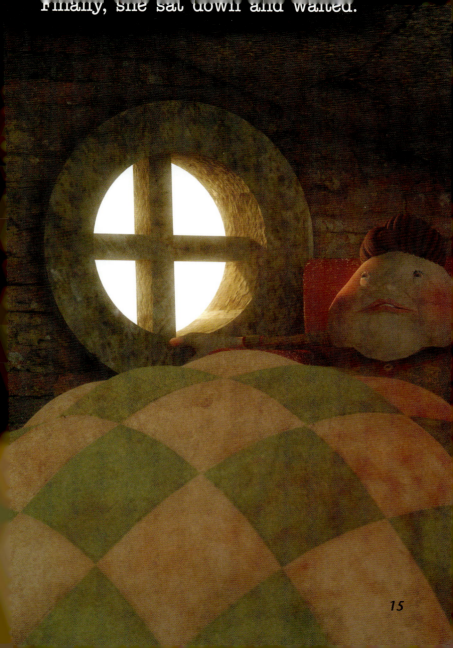

Finally, she sat down and waited.

The Giant's Causeway

Soon, Benandonner came storming into their cave, shouting, "Where's that feeble Finn? I'm ready to fight him!"

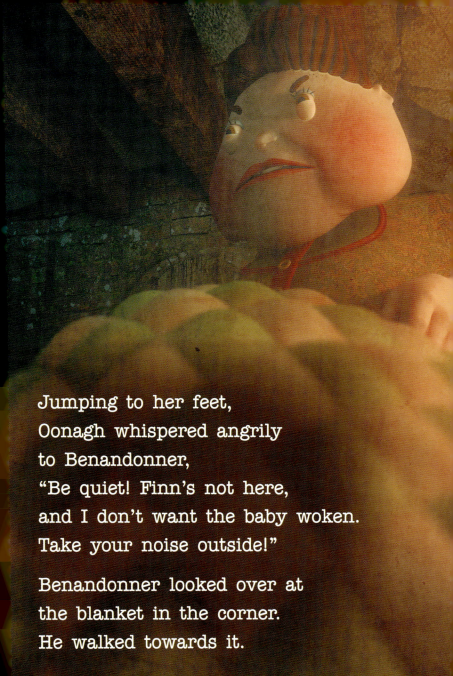

Jumping to her feet,
Oonagh whispered angrily
to Benandonner,
"Be quiet! Finn's not here,
and I don't want the baby woken.
Take your noise outside!"

Benandonner looked over at
the blanket in the corner.
He walked towards it.

The Giant's Causeway

Benandonner looked down
at the baby.
He couldn't believe it.
The baby was huge.
If the baby is this size,
what size is its father?
he thought.

He reached down to pat
the baby's head.
Finn bit Benandonner's hand
as hard as he could.
"Argh!" cried Benandonner.

"Now you've woken the baby!"
shouted Oonagh, rushing over.
"Wait until I tell his father
that you're over here
making trouble!
He'll be after you!"

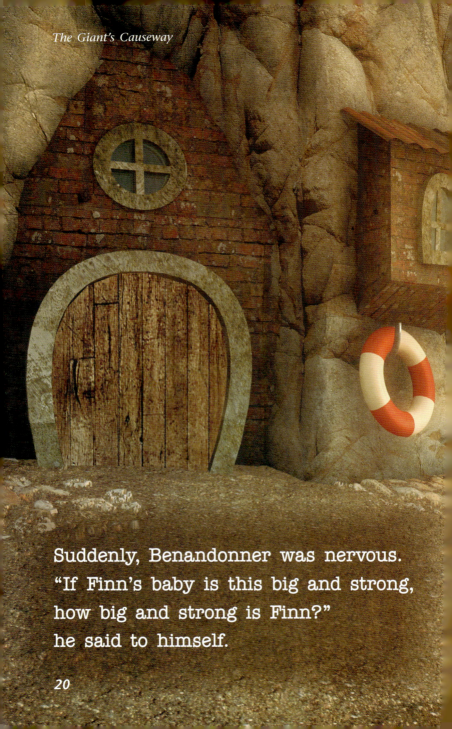

The Giant's Causeway

Suddenly, Benandonner was nervous. "If Finn's baby is this big and strong, how big and strong is Finn?" he said to himself.

Oonagh's Plan

He turned and ran back over the causeway, pulling up the rocks to stop Finn from coming after him.

Chapter 4
The Isle of Man

Finn and Oonagh started laughing as they watched Benandonner running back across the causeway.

Picking up some mud,
Finn threw it with all his might.
The mud missed Benandonner,
but it landed with a splash
close by.

The Giant's Causeway

After that, Benandonner never gave
Finn any more trouble.
He lived quietly in his cave in Scotland,
while Finn lived in his cave in Ireland.

The mud that Finn threw
at Benandonner
was named the Isle of Man.

the Isle of Man